Dedication

Ila, you are much better at rhyming than you were when we started this book. Of the thousands of books you've read, you've always said that you wanted more books with girls that look like you. I gave you the challenge of creating your own, and you came through in a big way. Now, little brown and black girls everywhere can see the positive images they truly represent and all kids can see realistic images of black girls. You are more than amazing! Not only are you brilliant, but you are also hard-working, talented and compassionate. I hope that you'll remember this book as the first of many pieces of work that tell *your* story. Your Dad and I are so proud of the work you've put into this book and your impeccable rhyming skills.

Special thanks to Jessica Morrow-Brand, whose consistent one word comment ("BOOK") on so many of my Facebook posts – encouraged us to write this book.

I'd like to also extend a heartfelt thanks to *my* Mom, Ether Frazier, for helping Ila Bean with the final prayer of this book.

- Mom

There were two sisters,
And then came me.
My parents were so happy
Because I made three.

My parents are kind and very smart.
My mom's best asset is her big heart.
My dad always keeps us on task.
Whatever we need, we simply ask.

My oldest sister nicknamed me "Ila Bean."
She said it was nice, but I thought it was mean.
Now, I love the name so much
Because she says it with just the right touch.

Énoa is her name and she has so much to do.
She loves cheer and studying - but mainly bossing us two.
She lets me tag along to get a mani-pedi,
And when she cooks – it's always spaghetti.

4

She shares her favorite things with me,
But it always comes with a small fee.
She makes me take her picture, so she can look tall.
But the truth is – she's really quite small.

She's in college, so no longer home with us.
It takes seven hours to reach her by bus.
I don't see her often, but that's okay.
I love her 'cause she lets me call her three times a day.

6

My older sister, Arí, was happy when I came along.
But the way she bosses me is just plain wrong!
She makes me floss my teeth and wrap my hair,
And get on my knees to say a prayer.

She holds my iPad until I clean my room.
She gives me so much math, I feel destined for doom.
She blames me for all the things she can't find,
And when she finds them, she says, "Nevermind!"

She's strict but has loved me since day one,
And when she relaxes, we really have fun.
She protects me whether I like it or not,
I guess that's why I love her a lot.

I know she wants me to do my best
And get a high score on every single test.
Being a big sister must be so much fun,
So, I wrote a prayer to get the job done.

"Now I lay me down to bed,
With just one thought in my head.
Lord, please help my parents to see
What a great big sister I would be."

I used to say this prayer every night,
And then one morning my dream came to light.
There he was licking my face.
We had a new puppy in this place!

He was warm and cute and soft as can be.
He was the perfect dog for a girl like me.
My "big sister" dream had finally come true.
My very first job was to rescue my shoe.

He is loving, cuddly, and chocolate-brown.
Nothing he does could make me frown.
He's always excited when I walk through the door.
And when I show him love, he shows me EVEN more.

I had to teach Nash lots of things.
You can't imagine the joy he now brings.
It took a while for him to sit and stay.
I was so happy when we reached that day!

He waits patiently while I read and write.
I think that's why he's super duper bright.
When my dad and I go outside to play catch,
I finally have a buddy who can run and fetch.

He really likes to play dress up.
I mean it when I tell you; Nash is such a good pup!
He loves me with all his heart.
Wearing sunglasses is his favorite part.

I love how he's patient with me.
He knows a vet is what I want to be.
I check his blood pressure every two weeks.
His puppy dog eyes are how he speaks.

Sometimes, I'm too tired to take him out.
But, I put on my shoes and try not to pout.
A great big sister, I will always be
Because his very existence depends on me.

If you become a big sister like me,
I hope you understand it's a big responsibility.
I get to teach him, feed him and take him for a walk.
Because I'm both loving and firm, he listens when I talk.

We spend most days just hanging out.
Showing love is what it's all about.
With him, I could never, ever be mean,
He's so excited when he hears "Ila Bean."

He's not allowed to sleep with me
It's important to set a boundary.
So, as Nash and I end each day,
I hug him tightly and head to my room to pray.

22

"Dear God,
Thanks for a dad who tucks me into bed,
Watch over Nash - keep him warm, safe and fed.
Guide my steps, so I'll always be fair.
Give my mom patience when she's combing my hair.
Bless my bossy big sisters even when we clash,
And don't forget to protect my best friend, Nash."

♡

Ila

Ericka Gibson

CPSIA information can be obtained
at www.ICGtesting.com
Printed in the USA
BVHW090441181119
564038BV00004B/37/P